The Gre Fragola Brothers

BY
JOE PRENDERGAST

March 2013

The Great Fragola Brothers
2013

Published by Emu Ink Ltd
www.emuink.ie

Cover Design by Ruth Mac Conville

ISBN: 978 - 1 - 909684 - 02 - 7

In support of

CANCER CLINICAL
RESEARCH TRUST

Dedication

For my wonderful, courageous, lovely Dad, who battled with
lung cancer for five and a half years. Geoff - 1960-2012.
And many thanks to my wonderful cuz Ruth,
who designed my fabulous first front cover.

March 2013

CHAPTER 1

The Great Fragola Brothers

The Great Fragola Brothers were preparing for their flight to LaGuardia Airport, from their native Venice. The airport was busy but they kept to themselves in the thronged building.

Paolo and Giuseppe Fragola were a magician act, which were very popular in their own part of the world but were travelling to New York to start their career abroad.

The two brothers, who didn't look at all alike, were similar in only one way and that was in their protectiveness of each other. Giuseppe was an undetermined amount of years older, as he would never reveal his age to anyone, and was known to be lazy and grubby. He wore a long coat with circles on it to cover up his unfashionable clothes and a cap to hide his scruffy hair while Paolo a vain, yet kind, 29-year-old wore smart outfits, put gel in his hair and couldn't resist a mirror – be he loved his brother more than anything.

Both men were eating cream doughnuts in a coffee shop called CUPPA in the airport and were deep in thought about what the next year would bring.

Though Paolo and Giuseppe lived in Italy, and had all their lives, they grew up learning English. Their mother was from Ireland and made sure they could speak English so, as a result, instead of Italian they tended to speak English most of the time.

The waitress gave Giuseppe a coffee, which he had been expecting for five minutes.

"Thank you," he said to the black-haired woman, then turning to his brother asked: "Paolo ever wondered what life is going to be like in New York?"

"Yes. I think it's going to be fun. I think people will like us," he said slouching in his chair, brown hair set perfectly and teeth whiter than white.

"I agree," said Giuseppe.

"I know you do. You agree with everything I say."

"Touché."

Both men laughed and relaxed in their seats.

"Do you think the children will like us?" Giuseppe pondered further.

"I think that they will love us. We are the most popular magician act in Venice and the most talked-about too, so everyone is following our every step."

Paulo paused: Will we like New York though?" he asked.

"We will enjoy it for the time being I suppose. It will get tedious after about a year I guess but then we will move somewhere else after that. Does that sound good?"

"Yes."

Giuseppe kept a close eye on the Departure Screen. It read; "LaGuardia New York. 17:00. Go to Gate."

It then repeated the title in Italian.

"Best be getting going."

"OK, Giuseppe."

So the two brothers made their way to Departure Gate five where there were fifty-one seats, and Giuseppe and Paolo took the last two.

Thirteen minutes later a booming voice came over the intercom. "Flight 1235579 to New York airport, LaGuardia, boarding."

The two men were twenty-third in the queue. Paolo liked to keep count of where they were in lines - or anywhere, really.

A woman with blonde curls reaching her shoulders and juicy-red lips took their passports, smiled ear to ear and said, "Welcome aboard!"

She ripped off part of their boarding cards and gave them back to Paolo and Giuseppe with a; "Enjoy your flight." Paolo noticed her name badge, which read Alice.

Quite taken he looked again at her after they had left. She did the same with every customer. 'Oh' he thought, a little disappointed and followed Giuseppe down the aisle to where they took their seats.

Paolo was skinny and had lightly tanned skin. He often wore a t-shirt which had the words; "IT'S MAGIC!" on it and he happened to be wearing it that day. He liked to advertise the fact that they were magicians.

He and his brother had started having an interest in showbiz about fifteen years previous and had started off their act as street-performers in Venice four years ago, after which they became increasingly popular, until, eventually, people were paying large amounts of money to see them.

One day, a German landlord name Josl Blieke – known for his amount of money –sat in the front row, paid much more than was needed for his seat and left with a quiet but snappy "Keep the change!"

The brothers were shell-shocked at the sight of all the money but they were also delighted as they were able to buy a building to use for the magic shows. They used this as their home as well.

Fashion magazines are overrated, Paolo thought to himself as he eyed the one in the pouch in front of him. Giuseppe was asleep.

There was no one to talk to and nothing good to read so he decided to try and sleep. And he did and when he woke up, or rather Giuseppe woke him up, the intercom's voice ended with the word descent.

"We're beginning our descent?" he asked groggily of his older brother.

"Yes. We will be there in five minutes. Got that?"

"Yeah, sure. How long did I sleep for?"

"A few hours."

"Wow. How long did you sleep for?"

"Less."

"Oh. Are you tired?"

"No, very energetic. You?"

"I'm okay. Looking forward to our beds though."

Paulo laughed, a sleep on a plane was never the same; "Yeah. But I'll be cool tomorrow."

"Brilliant."

All of a sudden they were touching down on the runway and it was sickening – the pilot was a newbie they guessed.

Paolo looked out of the window at the dazzling lights of New York.

"Oh, Giuseppe it's beautiful," he said, mesmerised.

"I know."

"How do you know?"

"Just, I do. OK!"

"OK! Calm down!"

Paolo looked further out at the many skyscrapers that were truly scraping the sky and smiled. He felt a jolt of happiness as the plane became slower and slower on the runway, until it eventually came to a halt.

Snow covered the place. It was nearly Christmas, and LaGuardia airport was busy.

A large shuttle bus was outside, bustling with people. Paolo and Giuseppe took their seats on the top of the bus and Paolo almost fell asleep only for the fact that their stop was the first one.

"Hello," said Giuseppe to the receptionist.

"Hi," he answered. "Hey, do you want the key for your room?"

"Yes, I believe we're number 311."

"Yeah, I have the key here."

He searched quickly for the key and about a minute later he produced a golden one with the words "THE NEW YORKER HOTEL, Room 311."

"Thank you."

"Hey, anytime!"

The brothers walked along the lobby to a large lift, which they guessed would fit about seven people. Giuseppe and Paolo, Paolo first, stepped into the lift and pressed 'Floor 3' – Bedrooms and the lift bolted off.

Seconds later there was a loud beep and the doors opened. In the doorway were three women, each with trunks full of things. They were checking out.

"This is it!" cried Giuseppe when they stepped into the fancy room. "This is Room 311! Yahoo!"

"I know, Giuseppe. This is where it all begins. Our proper career!"

"Let's get some sleep."

"Yeah."

So the two brothers found their pyjamas in the rucksacks that they had brought through the plane ride as hand luggage. They popped them on and found a bed each. They were in the beds about five minutes later, reading.

"Goodnight, Paolo."

"Goodnight, Giuseppe."

CHAPTER 2

"Ladies and Gentlemen..."

As two men – one twenty-nine and one thirty-ish – made their way to the restaurant connected to the hotel, a certain young actress was having breakfast, preparing for the big day ahead.

Dawn Hughes was a tall woman with curly blonde hair and red lips. She had big green eyes, unlike her sister Alice, who was an air-hostess. At the table, three people joined Dawn.

The first person, sitting opposite Dawn was a young man, she estimated he was two years younger than her – and he spoke with a Spanish accent. The person sitting beside him, Dawn knew well. He was Jacob Burke, her agent. He indicated to the man sitting beside him, who waved.

"This is Stephen Rice, the new big sensational director." Burke had curly black hair, was very casual, and was probably the kindest person ever to live on Earth - or at least that's what Dawn Hughes thought.

"Hello, Stephen," she replied, shaking Stephen's hand.

Next to Jacob was a girl that Dawn could tell was quiet and shy.

"Dawn. This is Polly O' Brien. She is from Dublin, Ireland and had applied to be your make-up artist."

The girl, Polly, looked about eighteen and was very interested in Dawn, who noticed immediately that she was stunningly beautiful.

Dawn sighed and the entire table enveloped themselves in breakfast. She wasn't very hungry so she didn't eat much. She spent her time, if the truth be told, just secretly staring at the amazing Polly O' Brien.

*

Paolo and Giuseppe took their seats in a large hotel restaurant, which was surprisingly beautiful. Paolo studied the menu he had been given thirty seconds earlier, scanning every inch of it.

"I think I'll get this," he said, pointing to a picture of a stack of pancakes. "Do you think it looks nice?"

"Mmm, looks lovely," Giuseppe licked his lips.

"I need something good. Today is a big day. Our first show…" His voice trailed off.

"I know! You know what we're going to do, right?"

"Yes, yes, I'm in on it. In fact, it was me who came up with it!"

A waiter came to the table and Paolo ordered, followed quickly by Giuseppe. When the waiter was finished taking down the order, he muttered a sort of "Thank you" and then scurried away.

*

The breakfast table was mostly silent, interrupted sometimes by Jacob trying to start a conversation. Dawn had thankfully taken her eyes off Polly.

"Polly," said Dawn, abruptly breaking the silence. "I would like you to be my make-up artist. I think you are the most beautiful girl I have ever seen in my life."

Polly's face lit up with a mixture of emotions - joy and happiness, a slight sadness, a worrying look and also what appeared to be sheer shock. "Oh, Ms Hughes! I'm so happy, so grateful, thank you! I could talk all day but I know you have business. I shall start right away," Polly said joyfully, and skipped off in the direction of the rooms.

"Now. Mr Rice," began Dawn.

"Yes senorita. Yes, miss?"

"Ah, how very impressive your English is. Anyway," Dawn found herself saying, "You're a director, right."

"Yes."

"And you… want to direct a movie with me in it?"

"Yes."

"Wow. OK, let me hear the idea for this film of yours."

"Well, I was thinking something like Jaws but with tigers."

"Oh! And what were you going to call it, Paws I'm guessing?" She gave a chuckle.

"Very funny, Miss," he attempted a laugh. "Now I'm talking man-eating tigers, trying to kill everyone. You see?"

"And who were you thinking I would play?"

A long pause followed.

"I was thinking you could play the tiger," said Paolo between mouthfuls of his pancake stack.

Giuseppe stopped eating his food and thought about this.

"Well if it means I don't have to play anything else, I'm fine with it."

"So you'll be the tiger?"

"Yeah."

"Great!"

The men finished off their breakfast and went back up to the room. "First show is at one. What time is it?" asked Giuseppe when they got back to the hotel room.

"Jeepers, it's already half past noon!"

"Let's get going then."

*

Dawn Hughes was watching Polly O' Brien who was on her Apple Mac laptop in Dawn's apartment; her screen-saver had just come up. There was a picture of a dog on the screen, pouting like crazy – Dawn presumed it was a family pet.

The mouse darted to an icon that read: 'Internet Explorer'. She double-clicked it and it opened up a large screen, with GOOGLE in the centre.

She started to type something in. It began with an S. Dawn looked away because she thought Polly would turn and see her.

She looked back when she was sure about Polly. SKYPE was the word she had typed in. The screen lit up with the login for Skype. She typed her user-name; mspollyobrien1 and then it entered her account.

Dawn was amused; she wanted to see who it was that Polly wanted to Skype. She watched as Polly selected the name Yvonne O' Brien.

Just then a large screen projecting a woman appeared – She had blonde hair that looked an awful lot like Polly's, and was in her late fifties-early sixties – Quite a lot of people joined this woman. There was a man in his twenties, two children who looked about nine and ten and a teenager, of about sixteen, with a terrier dog.

"Hello!" said Polly, clearly excited. "I got the JOB!!! And she said I am the most beautiful girl in the WORLD!!!"
"Oh, well done! Yes! YAY!" There was a lot of

excited chatter on the other end of the call.

Polly then looked at the dog on the screen. "Who's the greatest dog in the world, who's the greatest dog in the world? You are, Buzz. You are, Buzz!" she exclaimed.

The children started doing a disco dance, singing, "She got the job, she got the job," as they swung each other around in little circles.

The man in his early twenties smiled and said, "You did well, little sis!" and gave her the thumbs up.

The teenager said a quiet "Congratulations" before launching into questions about what Dawn was like.

"I don't know that much about her," laughed Polly. "Now, goodbye!" and she brought the quick call to an end.

"BYE! Well done! YAY!" the family said simultaneously before the screen went black.

Dawn turned and walked away before Polly turned around. Polly smiled. She was happy. She had done her family proud.

*

Paolo and Giuseppe left their hotel three minutes

after their discussion. They left in a flurry and were out into the snowy streets of New York in no time.

As they walked along, Paolo recited his lines, while Giuseppe just kept on repeating, "Everything is alright, everything is alright." He was clearly extremely nervous. Paolo sensed this but didn't feel in the mood to speak.

"Tigers first," said Paolo when they reached the venue. Giuseppe gave an almost silent chuckle and went inside. Ten seconds later he heard Paolo close the door behind him. "Here we are. We made it! Our first show in New York!"

*

Dawn noticed Stephen Rice in her kitchen, cooking some "Spanish cuisine" as he had mentioned earlier. She decided to check up on him – to make sure that the place wasn't on fire, more like.

She strode in to the kitchen. "Hello, Stephen. That isn't a very Spanish name. Well, if you think about it, Rice isn't either."

"My father was American."

"Ah, OK. Surely your father is American?"

"No, he died three years ago."

"Oh, I'm so sorry."

"Oh, no, it's fine. I mean, I'm fine."

"Good, because if I offended you in anyway,"

"No you didn't. Chill out. It's nothing."

"So, what Spanish cuisine are you cooking today for us?"

"Ah, I thought you'd prefer nothing. I really can't cook. I mean, I'm sorry if you were looking forward to it or anything."

It didn't smell like nothing.

"Let's talk business."

"OK, Dawn. What is it?"

"This movie about tigers, I want in on it. I considered it last night, and it's a brilliant idea. I will talk to you at 2 pm."

And before Stephen Rice could reply, she strode out of the room.

*

Paolo and Giuseppe Fragola went straight to the Ringmaster, a Sir Henry Bucket. He had hair that was neatly trimmed against his head and he was strikingly good-looking.

Paolo started off. "Hello, Sir Bucket."

"Ah, Paolo and Giuseppe! You're here. In about three minutes it should start.

And then Henry disappeared quickly and Paolo and Giuseppe were lead by four men in purple suits to the stage.

"Let the magic begin," the brothers shouted in unison and laughed.

*

After the show was over, with Giuseppe leading the way, they set off in search of a taxi.

"Taxi! Taxi!" shouted Giuseppe and a yellow car pulled up.

"Where to?" said the burly moustached man of a taxi-driver.

"The New Yorker Hotel, please."

CHAPTER 3

Filming with Tigers

Dawn Hughes sat in the back seat of a limo as it drove in the snowy weather to the set. The limo ground to a halt beside the building and Dawn thanked the driver and hopped out. The set was covered completely with a coat of snow and Dawn felt a shiver down her spine.

As she advanced forward, a certain man was watching her from the right. He was wearing a purple suit, was bald and two of his teeth were missing. A scar ran down his face. He snarled quietly at Dawn, but she did not hear. The door had just been opened and the figure of Polly O' Brien appeared before Dawn.

'Ah, one of my finest agents,' thought the man in the purple suit whose name was Victor Left. Victor was forty-five, but his thirst for money had started when he was sixteen years of age. He was never really a good kid and certainly wasn't a good adult. He had grown up with a hunger for being the most powerful man in the world and now employed millions of agents. Their colour was purple. They were working for Victor, for a lot of money in return.

He watched as Agent 6, Polly O' Brien, took the infamous Dawn Hughes into the set. He smiled. Polly was a brilliant agent, and was only just getting to show her skills then.

"Ah, Dawn!" exclaimed Jacob Burke.

"Jacob!" replied Dawn and they quickly hugged.

"So! You've talked to Stephen!"

"Yeah, I've talked to Stephen!"

The two began chatting and Polly O' Brien secretly sneaked outside, and through the alleyway.

"Ah, Agent 6. So nice to see you. You are doing your master proud."

Polly smiled. "I know."

The girl wasn't in fact that beautiful. It was all make-up.

"I know that you know, Ms O' Brien."

"That's it?"

"Oh, no," said Victor, quite taken aback by the question.

"Alright, then. What else have you to say?"

"You need to lure her into your room. Then, we – myself and Rook and Cranny, that is – will kidnap her. As simple as that. She is the biggest star on the planet and if we can manage to take her and hold her hostage the world will see how powerful we have become. It will instil fear and nations will have no choice but to succumb to my every wish for fear of what will happen to them. Then the Purple Army shall rule the world!"

At that the two of them erupted into tremendous evil laughs, filling the place with noise. "I shall, Master Left. I shall lure Dawn Hughes."

*

Paolo and Giuseppe sat down on their beds in The New Yorker Hotel. Paolo was reading Charles Dickens' A Tale of Two Cities while Giuseppe was reading Apollo 11: What Really Happened.

They were tired. The time was thirty or so minutes past seven o'clock, and soon they were to be going out for dinner. Paolo yawned and closed the book. Giuseppe did the same.

"Let's get going," said Giuseppe, getting up off the bed.

"Yeah, we should," replied Paolo and they got themselves ready.

About a half-hour later the two brothers made their way to reception as quickly as they could, saying hello to Dave, the kind man who was working at reception.

"On the way out to dinner I see," he said to Paolo.

"Yes, thank you," replied Paolo, walking after his brother and into the cold weather.

The two brothers found a restaurant named Columbia's Pizzeria, the home of the Pizza, where Giuseppe enjoyed a pizza while Paolo liked his pasta dish.

They ate silently. They were quite bored. The show was OK, it went down well enough.

"Hello!" came a voice, breaking the silence.

They turned around to see a woman. They recognised her immediately. "You're…"

"Dawn Hughes, famous actress," she said, doing sarcastic jazz hands. "At your service."

"Oh my God," said Giuseppe, enunciating each word. "It's… you're… DAWN!"

"Yes, I am. And I just noticed you. You look like nice guys… what brought you to New York?"

"Oh, just our career… we're magicians, so…"

"Oh, cool. Hey, do you think you could perform for me tomorrow?"

"Sure, where?"

"23rd Grange. Right next to The New Yorker."

"That's where we're staying!"

"Cool! See you around 3pm!"

"Sure, see you then, Dawn Hughes."

*

The next day Paolo and Giuseppe watched 23rd Grange, constantly, but Dawn never showed. Then, they saw an unusual thing.

Very unusual it was. Three men, all wearing purple suits, one ahead of the other two, began to stroll down the street. The man in front had a large scar running across his face. What Giuseppe and Paolo did not know, was that this was Victor Left.

The other two men – Samuel Rook and John

Cranny, two of the stupidest men on the earth, but also two of the strongest – looked like they were ready to use their full power.

"Giuseppe!" whispered Paolo, but he was already beside him. "Shush, Paolo. He might hear us."

"OK, I'll shut up."

"Good."

The three men walked along the street until they came to 23rd Grange.

"What are they doing?" whispered Paolo to Giuseppe.

"Oh, you think I'll know?" he replied sarcastically.

"Never mind," Paolo waved his hand at his brother.

They watched as the door opened and standing there was not Dawn Hughes, but a younger, beautiful girl.

"Hello, Polly," said the man, standing in front, with the scar.

"Hello Victor. You wanted … Dawn."
Paolo and Giuseppe's faces froze as Dawn Hughes, in all her beauty, and with her eyes fixated on Victor Left, came out and before Dawn or Polly could say

anything Victor pulled out a large bag and put it completely over Dawn, after which all Paolo and Giuseppe could hear were her desperate screams and shouts.

Victor then picked her up and walked back the way they had came, Rook and Cranny hot on his heels as he shouted over his shoulder to Polly "Thank you for your service, Agent 6. I'll raise your payments by five per cent."

"No, Master Left. Thank you."

And with that, Polly O' Brien and Victor Left went their separate ways.

Paolo and Giuseppe watched in awe as the most famous actress ever was taken away by the leader of The Purple Army.

*

That night, when they were in their beds, Giuseppe said something crazy. "I think we should go find her."

"What? Are you crazy?"

"No! I think we should go find Dawn Hughes!"

CHAPTER 4

After The Kidnapping

Paolo's face showed a mix of anger, surprise, sheer shock and curiosity. Giuseppe suddenly regretted what he had said. No one would go with him. Or would they?

"Are you crazy?" asked Paolo again, eyeing him as if that statement was true.

"No, I'm not crazy!" retorted Giuseppe.

"Giuseppe! Think about what you're saying! Think about what Mama would say. We are quiet people. We don't interfere with other people, you hear me?!" shouted Paolo, a little louder than he intended.

Giuseppe stopped abruptly. He was clearly upset. Paolo was about to say, "Giuseppe, I'm sorry" but it was Giuseppe's turn to say something.

"I am going to find Dawn Hughes. If you don't want to come with me, that's completely fine, I don't care, but I am going to look for Dawn Hughes and I am going to find her. I swear."

Giuseppe then stood up and left the room.

Paolo got to his feet and followed silently as Giuseppe walked down the stairs to reception and sat there.

Paolo approached him and said; "Giuseppe, I'm sorry. May I please join you to find Dawn? Please."

Giuseppe's face lit up. "You really would?" he asked in disbelief.

"Yes, of course. You're my brother and I love you."

"Aw… Come here," and the two men hugged.

"Um, kind of trying to save Dawn Hughes here," Giuseppe started to laugh.

"Oh, yeah. I better put my game face on, cause we have a lot of work to do."

"You can say that again."

"I better put my game face on, cause we have a lot of work to do."

"Not literally."

"Oh," and they laughed again.

Dawn was cramped in a pitch-black cell with no windows. It could have been morning, afternoon, evening. It could have been night. She didn't know if she'd been in there only ten minutes, or if she'd been in there ten hours. She was clueless as to what was going on.

The last thing she saw of some importance was the man with the scar in the purple coat – the one who kidnapped her. As she mulled over what had brought it about, her shock at Polly's betrayal, she heard footsteps coming down into the cell.

In an instant she could almost make out an extremely tall man but could not distinguish who it was until she saw the red scar across his face. It was the man who took her. She tried to say something, but her lips were frozen with fear.

She moved. Thankfully Victor had problems with hearing and wasn't alerted to it. She felt safe for now but then the cold started to kick in. It was freezing. She tried to stop her teeth chattering but she couldn't.

Unfortunately, Victor just happened to be passing the doorway of her cell at that instant and he stopped abruptly and gave a loud cackle.

"Ah, Ms Dawn. I see you've arrived to your cell

safely," he smiled and paused before adding… "For now."

*

Giuseppe and Paolo went back up to the room to think about what they were going to do.

They struggled to stay awake as they tried to think of a plan for saving Dawn. Waking up Paolo who had eventually nodded off, Giuseppe said "A search party!" and Paolo shot upright.

"You mean other people?"

"Yes, I mean other people."

"That's brilliant. Dawn Hughes is so popular that everyone will want to help save her!"

"Yeah, I know. That's the whole point."

"Oh ok. I get it, I get it."

It was all they needed to put their minds at ease and the two brothers fell into a dreamless sleep.

*

"Victor? Victor … Victor…" Dawn knew a Victor once..but…no it couldn't be…

"Left, Dawn. Yes. It is I, Victor Left. I don't know if you remember me."

"All these years…" her mind was racing…

"Yes. All those years we spent together. I even considered proposing to you but never mind. You just had to become a star, and leave me on my own. I had to pay all the rent."

"What? I did not leave you. I arranged to meet you that night, the one before I left. You did not show. I thought that you didn't love me anymore. So I left and cried every night for a month…" Tears were glistening on Dawn's face.

"I am not going to harm you but if someone comes along to save you, I will request money. And lots of it, I assure you. People need to know of my power. If I can get a hold of the world's most famous actress and demand a ransom they will fall at my feet and the world will be mine."

Dawn felt she had no choice. What's more she felt she didn't know Victor anymore and so she decided the best thing to do was not to argue.

"Alright, but I refuse to live in this little cramped cell," she said, knowing she was chancing her luck.

"Well, I'm afraid you'll have to like it," he barked

and with that he walked out and slammed the door.

Suddenly Dawn started to cry. "Goodbye Victor. Victor Left."

"Goodbye Dawn," she could hear him whisper on the other side of the door.

*

When Paolo woke the first thing he thought about was the search party. Then he recollected the recent events that shook him and his brother's "career holiday" to New York. He was scared. He felt stupid that he had dragged them into this mess in the first place.

It was going to end, and it probably wasn't going to end well.

Paolo shook Giuseppe's shoulder and the man sat upright.

"Morning Paolo," said Giuseppe, remembering the past events too.

"Morning Giuseppe," replied Paolo. "How did you sleep?"

"Like a log."

"Oh, that's good. So, the search party?"

"Oh, yeah."

"So, who should we ask?"

"I dunno. Why don't we ask Dave at reception?"

"OK. Let's go then."

The two brothers made their way down to the lobby where Dave Brackett, in his morning suit, was just sitting there, unoccupied, and smiling.

"Hello, boys," he said as Paolo and Giuseppe walked into the room. "Hi Dave. Could we speak to you in um, private?" asked Paolo.

"Yeah, sure," said Dave, quickly getting up off his chair and joining the two brothers. "But make it quick."

"Where should we…?"

"Follow me."

The two men, with the least bit of reluctance, followed the American receptionist down the hall of The New Yorker Hotel.

They reached a door with a golden plate, which had

the word 'Office,' emblazoned on it in black lettering.

"Come on," beckoned Dave, and the two brothers stepped into the room.

It was a lovely room. The Persian carpet was irresistible, the couches made of fine Italian leather.

In the middle of the room was a desk. Though a person could hardly see it – it was covered in crazy things haphazardly thrown about the place.

Paolo looked closer and guessed that most of the things were antiques.

There were shelves everywhere too, in every corner, hiding behind every couch, everywhere! The shelves were again filled with antiques, some trophies thrown in, and a lot of paperwork strewn about.

Finally, Dave spoke. "So you're probably wondering why the hotel's office is like this, right?"

Paolo nodded slowly and Giuseppe said; "Yes."

"Well, we're not really a hotel."

"What?"

"Fine. I suppose I have to tell you everything."

"We'd quite like that, if you don't mind."

"Well, the hotel is just the city base for our secret society. We've been working here for nearly a hundred years now. We are named The Three Circles. But before I tell you more, you must promise you will not tell anyone of our secret service. Both of you," he said, eyeing Giuseppe.

"I promise."

"I promise."

"Good," said Dave. "If that is the case then I will tell you and perhaps be able to help you out with whatever problem you appear to have."

CHAPTER 5

The Tale of Three Circles

"Let me begin," said Dave, looking at the Fragola Brothers in a very grave way. "By telling you that long ago, in 1912, a man started the Three Circles, a league of top secret agents. 'Why he did this?' you ask.

"Well I'll tell you. About two years before that, another service had started; The Purple Army. Now recently, they have captured the famous Dawn Hughes under the direction of the evil Victor Left, the Army's current leader. That's what you were coming here to tell me yes?"

He paused as the brothers, staring open-mouthed, nodded in silence.

"I know everyone and everything," Dave said in explanation. "I am the Chief Assistant of the head of The Three Circles Society, a Ms Rose Dahlia, who I am sure you two will be meeting soon – but, I digress."

Taking a deep breath he continued: "This service was set up to put an end to The Purple Army, which we have not yet done. They are up to something, and it's The Three Circles duty to stop them. Though I might seem like a normal receptionist, there is more to me than meets the eye. You'll see."

At that point Dave, who was fairly small in height, stopped for breath while Paolo and Giuseppe stood there, dumbstruck.

"For God's sake, don't just stand there and stare at me," he eventually said to Paolo and Giuseppe and gestured to some chairs.

"As I was saying, you'll see. When will you see? Soon, you will see. I know that you want to put together a search party. Don't worry. The whole of The Three Circles can handle that."

"Glad that that's sorted," said Paolo, who had simply decided to not believe Dave, sarcastically.

Unfazed Dave looked at him: "If you want to find Dawn Hughes, you have to trust me. If you do not, the whole world will be enslaved by the power of Victor Left. The world, as we know it, will end, because people will give in. Rather than risk his wrath, they will succumb to his power and we are the only ones able to stop it."

"And how's that?" Paolo remained suspicious.

"We are The Three Circles society. If something bad goes down, we all rally around. For instance, if Giuseppe here," – he indicated to the man – "were to be kidnapped, we would all search for him."

"And may I ask where the rest of you are?"

"Ah. I knew you would ask that question. Well, I shall show you. Follow me."

The two brothers followed Dave down the hall and to another door marked: Cellar.

Dave opened the door and inside there was a ladder, which he began to climb down. It was old and covered in cobwebs. Some dead flies were scattered about. It was gross and dangerous but if Paolo and Giuseppe wanted to know more, they would have to follow Dave and climb down the ladder.

Giuseppe went first, being very careful as he climbed. Paolo followed, scurrying down to get it over with. The room below was pitch-black.

"Now," continued Dave, "Where was I? Oh yes, you were going to meet the rest of the gang, right?"

"Yep," replied Giuseppe.

"Then let's go."

The three men kept walking to where there was another downward ladder. "Go on," said Dave, and the three climbed down one after the other.

"Where are we?" asked Paolo. They had been walking for about a minute when they came to a door. This one was not marked. Dave opened it and turned around before Paolo or Giuseppe could peek to see what the room was like. "Welcome to HQ."

As he said it Paolo and Giuseppe just knew, that after this moment, that their lives would never be the same again. The things they were about to see would change them forever. It was true and now they had a tiny spark of hope that Dawn would be returned safely.

The people in the room were obviously important – though most of them looked like they weren't exactly up with the fashion. Their clothes looked like items that Italian landlords might have worn in the 1600s. Paolo and Giuseppe nearly laughed at the group of bizarrely dressed people in front of them.

"What is it?" asked one of them – a pretty red-haired girl who looked around fifteen, the magicians thought.

"Just … what you're wearing," replied Paolo, stifling a laugh. The girl lunged at him, but Dave stepped in front of her. "Vivian! Be nice to our guests. You too, Daniel."

Dave indicated a boy, about a year older than the feisty Vivian, who was busy combing his hair and staring at himself in the mirror.

The other people – there were about twenty in total – smiled and some even waved and said "Hello."

Then Dave took to introducing. He swept across the room to Vivian. "This," he began, "Is Vivian Brackett. She is the granddaughter of the founder of The Three Circles, Henry Brackett. She's our youngest agent."

Then Dave went to the boy named Daniel. "This is Daniel Diamond. He is the sixteen year old, friend/ occasional enemy of Vivian. They will show you around the castle."

"The castle!" said Paolo, amazed by the whole thing.

"Yes, there is an invisible castle within the walls of the hotel," Vivian said sarcastically.

"No, you'll have to drive to Mahogany Castle," said Dave giving her a 'have manners' look. "It's not so far away and it's our home base. You'll be fine. Don't worry."

Daniel and Vivian started walking to the exit and Paolo and Giuseppe followed eagerly after them.

They had only walked for around ten seconds, which brought them to a large door at the back of the room. Pushing it open Vivian said: "We'll just get you to the car. It's waiting outside. Come on," she said, beckoning Daniel and the two men.

An old Bentley, blue in colour with what looked like a British registration – Paolo was not one to judge – sat out the back. They hopped into the 1950s car and, driver in place; it sped off at its top speed… which was painfully slow.

About twenty minutes later they turned onto a road and something caught the brothers' attention.

They had passed a sign that read: 'Welcome to Mahogany Castle'. Of course the sign was so old that ivy had grown all over it, and you could barely make out what it said, but it was there all the same.

What surprised Paolo and Giuseppe was that a gargantuan fence bordered the whole place. A sign that had been slightly torn off blew in the wind. It read: Shut down Due to Paranormal Activity. Paolo shuddered, and the car moved on to the fence.

Then, before their very eyes, the fence opened in a square shape, and the car passed through. Then it closed again after them.

Giuseppe and Paolo were quite bewildered by the

whole thing but there was no time to ponder because all four of them were to get out of the car immediately.

As they each hopped out the chauffeur quickly gave them a wave, which Daniel returned, and then they were on their way to the daunting-looking gates of the castle.

*

Dawn Hughes was cramped in her cell and she did not like it one bit. What she imagined to be a whole day had passed, and the pit of her stomach was beginning to lose to nerves.

At that very moment, she was telling herself they were planning something and the only good thing to happen was that Victor Left had said that he wouldn't harm her.

He was an old friend of hers, and they had once gone out with each other, but it ended in a total disaster.

These days, she pondered, she was a different person. She had made decisions and become a success but, if the truth were told, she hated it. She felt like being a kid again, being carefree, not an actress. Oh, she loved it at the start, but each day it became more and more tiring until it finally became unbearable.

She dreaded going to the studio each day, but she put up with it – if she backed down now, she would never forgive herself for regretting it, even if, for now, she despised all of the attention. Her life was chaos. Most days she would walk out of her house to hundreds of camera lights flashing at her and comments from gossip-magazine journalists whirling around in her brain like a tornado. Such intrusion.

Still, she thought of her family, and how they had gone from being awfully poor to being the most famous family in the world, all because of her. She couldn't quit being an actress now, and watch her family go back to living on the streets with not a penny in their pockets.

Her final thought before sleep caught up with her was; You will get out of here, Dawn. You will get out. Somebody will come and get you.

*

The decorations on the door of Mahogany Castle were extremely interesting. Some looked like the heads of Greek Gods, others were, simply, various shapes but one, in particular, caught Paolo's eye. The symbol, three circles within each other. It was obviously the symbol of The Three Circles Society.

Vivian, who was leading the group, grabbed the large brass doorknob in the centre of the door. She cranked it eight times – Paolo was counting. Then the doors swung open, and Daniel and Vivian stepped inside.

Paolo and Giuseppe followed into a hallway shrouded in darkness but peppered by quick flashes of light every once and a while.

Paolo heard Vivian's footsteps, and then she pulled on something, which triggered a light that brightened the whole room.

Paolo and Giuseppe nearly had to close their eyes before they got their first glimpse of the inside of the beautiful castle.

The first thing that both men noticed was the skylight. There were decorative tiles – all with that symbol, the three circles – which led to twelve panels where sunlight shined in easily.

Bookshelves were everywhere down the long corridor. Some books, because of the way in which they were piled on top of each other, looked like they were about to break at the spine and fall to the ground.

Statues and more crazy ornaments surrounded the bits the bookshelves didn't cover. The carpet was white – a bit stained, but still white – and in the middle of the hall was a fountain around which were four stone benches. There were doors everywhere and a winding staircase that, despite being behind the fountain, was more than capable of being seen.

The room smelled of a strange combination of roses and frying bacon, old books and chlorine with a slight hint of lemonade.

Vivian sat down on one of the benches.

"Welcome to Mahogany Castle, base of The Three Circles Society," she said rather grandly.

"This is the grand entrance and there are twelve rooms which I am going to show you around."

Then hopping up off the bench as quickly as she sat down she added: "Next room. One down, twelve to go."

CHAPTER 6

Mahogany Castle

Of the thirteen rooms, including the grand entrance, of Mahogany Castle, Paolo's favourite was the second one they came to. It was the banquet hall. In the middle, and surrounded by yet more ornaments, bookshelves, and this time portraits – was a large dining table that was ten metres long and covered in silver plates filled with rich food imported from all over the world.

Sitting in the twenty seats were another twenty people, this time dressed like old-fashioned Englishmen. One of them stood up. He was a thin man in his early fifties, wearing a pinstriped suit with tails, and a bowler hat.

"Ah, darling Vivian. Daniel, I see you're joining us today," he certainly spoke with a British accent. "These are the new fellows, I see. The Fragola Brothers, am I correct?" asked the man, turning to Paolo and Giuseppe.

"Yes, this is Paolo and Giuseppe," Vivian answered cheerily.

"Oh, spiffing! May I speak frankly?"

"Yes, you may."

"Oh, jolly good!"

Suddenly his demeanour changed and the warmth he initially exuded disappeared. Now he was very grave. "I think that … if you all work together, and quickly, to find out the whereabouts of this Dawn Hughes, you can save her. You must."

With that they left, walking quickly along a tiled corridor and to the next room.

"Who was that?" Giuseppe asked Vivian.

"A long-serving member of The Three Circles," she said simply.

*

Daniel took over the place of tour guide leading into the third room, the living room. Straight in front of them when they walked in was a fire, red flames lighting up the room.

There were a few settees, quite uninteresting but nothing more than that. Only when they were about to leave, however, did something catch Paolo's eye. A trinket was lying on the floor. It was some sort of bracelet, with decorations engraved on it. The symbol of The Three Circles appeared again, it was everywhere. These people clearly meant business, he thought.

The Three Circles were obviously serious about finding Dawn. It simply was going to happen, whether Victor Left liked it or not. The fate of the world – well, sort of… - depended on it!

"Next room!" shouted Vivian melodramatically. She was back on form, and they walked on to the fourth room. "The kitchen!"

This was Giuseppe's favourite room. It was filled with interesting aromas and it wasn't nearly as crowded as the banquet hall. There was one man, bossing around five other men, who smiled when he saw Vivian.

"Ah, 'ello Vivian."

"Hello, Cook. What are you making today?"

"I think I'm making a stew – Nathaniel left. Claim's his wife's 'aving a baby. Don't believe 'im."

"You've got to let him off the hook. He's only a rookie."

"It's 'ard, but I'll try."

"Good, now Cook… I'd like you to meet The Great Fragola Brothers."

Cook was a fat man with a big bushy moustache that curled over his mouth. He had a warm smile and rosy cheeks, but something about him was slightly harsh.

He was wearing a stripy apron over something that you would see a builder wear. He looked like he was dedicated to food, even from a distance.

When he was younger, he ran a pizzeria back in Paris but it shut down due to the fact that no one ate there. Then he move to America, became involved with The Three Circles, and for ten years had been the head chef, Cook, as he was known. His real name was Philippe Cain – "Raising Cain", as his teachers in primary school knew him – he was always making trouble.

He smiled his lovely smile and laughed his fruity laugh at the boys, before formally introducing himself. They shared a few words about Dawn and life, and then they left the kitchen.

About a minute later the small group reached a staircase. It was nothing like the huge staircase at the grand entrance – this was more of a back staircase and at it was a brass door. Daniel opened this.

"Room five," said Vivian and they stepped in.

Room Five was exceptional. It was full of something that surprised everyone. Balloons. They were big and small, every colour you could imagine and they were floating across the room.

There wasn't much the group could do but look on in awe. There was no room for them to step inside, without the danger of getting lost in the sea of colour, so after a few minutes they set off again.

The party walked out of Room Five and up the winding staircase. At the top, there was a long, well-lit corridor that led to a wall. A dead end. Finished. Completely finished. A dead end.

All of a sudden Vivian shouted something – too quickly for anyone else to here – and a door appeared. Daniel turned a bright, yellow doorknob in the middle of the green-coloured door, and they stepped through the previously dead end.

The room had a lovely smell – like roast chicken, but it had nothing to do with food. This was obviously some sort of old-fashioned weapon storage space.

The gang walked onwards and soon, in introduction, Vivian was shouting: "The weapons room!"

It was amazing. Unlike most rooms, it was completely bare except for a large cabinet and in this cabinet rested a large array of weapons from down through the ages.

They included crossbows, modern-day guns, axes, swords and about any other weapon you could ever think of or even make up.

Vivian smiled a wide smile and then took to speaking about the origins of the room.

"This room was one of the first rooms that my grandfather built. There isn't much too it, very bare but it served a huge purpose. It is the most secure room in the house - it has to be to house all this stuff. I love it, only because it has played a big part in the castle's, and therefore my, history."

"It was built in 1914. My grandfather was a young man – about thirty-six, and he'd built two rooms previously. This was the third." She stopped to take a breath, looked around the room once more.

Paolo could have sworn she was about to cry, but sensing he was watching; she stopped dead and continued speaking. "Well, no lollygagging – on to the next room!"

The group did as they were told. The next door was surprising in colour. It was pink! With a green doorknob that was yanked by Daniel, and the door opened.

"Room seven. The dressing room!" said Daniel, leading the way. It was obviously his favourite room. He admired everything. There was only one person in the room, amidst the clothes, hidden.

This person stepped out. It was a man with long dreadlocks – he looked like he was Jamaican – who was fussing over clothes.

"Sinbad!" shouted Daniel at him, and the man turned around.

"Daniel!"

"Sinbad, how are you?"

"Good!"

"I haven't seen you in an age!"

"I know! I was at the catwalk in Germany!"

"Brilliant! How did it go?"

"Brilliantly! It was amazing!"

"Oh, these two men," Daniel suddenly remembered himself and indicated Paolo and Giuseppe, "are The Great Fragola Brothers. They are here on the Dawn Hughes kidnapping front. You in on it?"

"Chief said she's gonna give me some more info, but for now – without a clue."

"When's she giving you the info?"

Sinbad checked his watch. "Actually now!"

"Go then!" Daniel almost shouted. "And we'll be in the main room when you're finished!"

"Okay!" Sinbad shouted back, and he disappeared down the hallway.

"We should probably move on. Room eight!" shouted Daniel and he led the way.

The next room was the music room, which had orange tiles lining the floor. A few instruments were lying around and some odd trinkets sat on the bookshelves.

"The music room was built in 1920, for the musical geniuses of The Three Circles Society to play in," explained Daniel.

"Don't really like this room, do you Daniel?" asked Vivian.

"It's not all that bad … but it doesn't … catch your eye," he replied.

"Mmm."

"Next room!"

The four of them walked out of the music room and on to another brown door.

"Banquet hall 2!" said Daniel.

This room was pretty much the same as the other Banquet Hall apart from the fact that this one was deserted with the exception of one person.

He was wearing a suit and a tie, and he had a thick mass of curly blond hair. He looked like he was in his early twenties. His face showed an expression of solemnity. He was obviously important and ate in a hurry.

The arrival of the four of them did not seem to disturb him whatsoever. He stayed there for a long time, not saying anything, but eventually stood up.

He walked over to Paolo, Vivian, Giuseppe and Daniel and looked at them.

"You probably don't know who I am, do you?" he asked Daniel.

"No," Daniel admitted.

"I am Claus Van Helsingr – I work for Rose."

"Ah, I see. Are you here on important business?"

"No."

"Then I suggest you leave right away."

The man, Claus Van Helsingr, walked away slowly, going back the way Paolo and Giuseppe and the others had come.

"Who does he think he is?" whispered Daniel to Vivian.

"He works for Rose, so I advise you shut up!" Vivian whispered back.

They then left the room, walking on to the tenth room they'd seen so far.

It was starting to get a bit tedious for The Fragola Brothers, but they tagged along. The next room was the office of this so-called Rose.

There was a tidy desk in the middle of the room. Sitting at that tidy desk was a woman with straight hair and an even straighter expression.

She looked up and said "Hello."

"Hello, Ms Dahlia," replied Daniel for the group.

"Daniel. Actually, it's good to see you. I was just about to go looking for you two. Or rather, four."

"Is this on the Dawn Hughes front?"

"Yes, I'm afraid so." She looked solemnly at Paolo and Giuseppe.

"Alright, what is it?"

"We have some… information."

"Uh-uh…"

"We know where she is. She is in a run-down hardware store in Southern Brooklyn."

"How did you find all of this out?"

"I know people."

"OK. I hear you were talking to Sinbad."

"Yes. He's knows everything. He's willing to try the best he can."

"Good. We'll need all the help we can get."

"I know. Now, I have stuff to be doing. Lovely meeting you all."

The four of them moved out of the room, and on to

Room 11.

This room was just another living room. A few trinkets lying around, nothing interesting. The fire wasn't on which was strange as the castle was very cold.

"Why isn't that fire blazing?" asked Paolo.

"Just…because," replied Vivian, striding out of the room. She was good at making mystery where, the magicians suspected, there was no real mystery at all.

The next room was another office. It was obviously that of a deputy. He wasn't there. His name was JJ Bines according to the sign on the door.

When they came to the thirteenth, Vivian and Daniel kept on walking. "Why don't we go in?" asked Giuseppe.

"You don't have to go in!" shouted Vivian, her face now red with anger. The tears came flooding out of her. Then she stopped, abruptly and said gravely "Don't ever go into that room. Ever."

*

Dawn Hughes lay down in her cramped cell. Someone will come. I just have to be patient. Someone will come to save me. And they will come soon.

CHAPTER 7

Volunteers

The Fragola Brothers woke to smells of frying bacon and scrambled eggs. They sat up in their twin beds, examining the room they were sleeping in. It was a high-ceilinged room with small trinkets lying around. There was a portrait of a woman who looked a lot like Rose, but it was not. It was her mother – it said so underneath the portrait.

Giuseppe got up out of the bed. He began to walk out of the room when Paolo said, "Where are you going?"

"I smell food, and close," he answered.

"OK, I'll come with you."

Paolo hopped out of the bed and quickly joined Giuseppe. They walked out of the bedroom and followed the smell down the hall. It was quickly becoming clear that they were back in the hotel, home to the secret HQ of The Three Circles Society. The smell eventually led them into the kitchen and there, cooking, was Dave and Vivian while Daniel, and the others from the previous day, were sat at a table.

"G'morning, Paolo and Giuseppe," said Dave cheerily. They realised they hadn't seen him since they left him the day before.

"Morning."

"Morning Dave."

The two men took their seats and were served with fried bacon that smelled like food heaven, two fried eggs each, some scrambled eggs, toast, beans, hash browns, and a rich sauce that The Fragola brothers had never heard of.

They ate like pigs – and for a very long time. They were ravenous. No one spoke as they were too busy eating and after breakfast was finished the team (Dave, Paolo, Giuseppe, Vivian and Daniel) hopped into the blue Bentley and headed off to Mahogany Castle to get a plan together.

The Bentley was slow. Very slow. Extremely slow in fact. So slow that even Vivian got frustrated.

It took twenty minutes, again, to get to Mahogany Castle, which Paolo and Giuseppe knew very well by now so they weren't too fazed.

The gang walked from the courtyard to the doors, which were opened by Vivian. When they walked in they were surprised to find that the grand entrance hall was full of people chatting and drinking champagne.

When Vivian spotted Sinbad amongst the crowd she asked "What's going on?" and Sinbad replied.

"The Lord Mayor of Mahogany has finally allowed us to use Mahogany Castle legally."

"Wow. That's brilliant. But what about the Dawn Hughes case. Doesn't anybody care about that?"

"Um…yes, if you count you five. I would love to help, but I'm kind of busy."

"Okay." She was stunned and a little annoyed but added, "Listen, I'll see you around, Sinbad."

"See ya, Vivian."

The group walked onwards and bumped into Rose Dahlia who was surprised to see them.

"Oh, why hello, Vivian, Daniel, Paolo, Giuseppe and," She looked surprised to see Dave there. "Dave. What are you doing here?"

"The Dawn Hughes case, Ms Dahlia. If you don't mind, I'll be on my way."

Dave walked on, showing his back to Rose. The other three followed him closely.

Dave in front, behind him was Vivian, behind Vivian was Paolo, and lagging a little bit further behind were Daniel and Giuseppe.

"What was that all about?" Giuseppe asked.

"What?"

"Rose and Dave."

"Oh. I'll tell you. He was meant to be the chief, but Rose beat him to it."

"Ah. I see."

"Yeah, he kind of makes a big show of it too."

*

Victor Left was sitting in a green armchair in a unique looking room. It had a green carpet with a blue ceiling and a purple wardrobe stood in the corner. A few Picasso-like paintings hung from nearly every wall.

Victor liked this room. He was pleased with himself, and very. He had captured Dawn Hughes, with the help of the girl who was with him in the room. He now regarded Polly O' Brien as one of the Purple Army's finest agents.

It was Victor Left's intention to leave Dawn Hughes in her cell underneath the run-down hardware store in Brooklyn and wait for The Three Circles Society to come to her rescue. When they did he would threaten to kill her unless they gave him a lot of money, more money than you could imagine, and when they did he would let her go. Either way he was going to look like the most powerful man in the world, with the most money, and at the same time he would spare the woman he once loved (and, in truth, still did) without them knowing he even cared.

It took them weeks to put their plan into action. It was fool proof, he believed but what The Purple Army did not know was that a lot of people from The Three Circles would come, but they wouldn't be giving a lot of money.

*

During the day, Paolo and Giuseppe, along with Dave, Vivian and Daniel, searched the town of Mahogany for willing participants to descend on the hardware store where they now knew Dawn to be.

It was late afternoon and they had already gathered fifteen people. They had until sunset, which wasn't far away, since it was winter.

There was one hour left to find more people and they were two minutes into that hour when six people walked by. They were businessmen, by the looks of it. They were all wearing the same outfit – a grey plaid suit with a green tie.

The men approached the foursome. "William and Co," they said, stating the name of their business.

"And what have you got to do with anything?" said Dave, a little impatiently.

"We hear you're looking for volunteers for the search of Ms Dawn Hughes. We'd like to help."

"OK. Do you know Mahogany Castle?"

"Uh, that creepy place? Yeah. Why?"

"Meet us there."

"What?"

"I said meet us there."

"Man, you're crazy!"

"Do you want to find Dawn Hughes?"

"Yes."

"Then I suggest you meet us at Mahogany Castle at four o'clock! And don't be late!"

"Ok, see you then."

"Good."

Then off walked the six men. Now they had twenty-one people in a search party.

They were doing well. It was just two minutes to four when they had finally gathered thirty people. They then walked back up the hill and into Mahogany Castle, to await the arrival of the thirty extra searchers.

About one minute later the whole group crammed into Room Five, which was no longer filled with balloons. They sat down.

There were twenty-nine chairs, which didn't matter as Dave was stood on a podium that made him look like a politician running for president.

The group shared their life stories and explained why they would be useful in the rescuing.

Then, abruptly, stopping all the speeches, Rose Dahlia strode in.

"Hello Rose," said Dave, not as awkwardly as before but awkward all the same. "Is there anything you'd like to say?"

"Yes."

"And what is that?"

"I would like to say that I will not be joining you in your mission."

"Oh, alright then. Why not?"

"Because I have things to do and places to go and people to see in those places."

"Okay, goodbye then."

"Good day."

"Right back at you."

Then Rose left the room, and the meeting continued.

Another speech was made, which certainly wouldn't be the last.

CHAPTER 8

Preparation

When the meeting was finished, Paolo and Giuseppe met with JJ Bines outside the castle.

"So I hear you're the Deputy Head," said Giuseppe, as Paolo walked on.

"Oh, yeah, I am," shrugged humble JJ.

"Cool."

"Yeah, it's OK."

"Don't you like being Deputy?"

"Um… let's just say it's not as good as people expect it to be."

"But you're the Deputy Head of a secret society."

"Actually, I hate it." His voice dropped to a whisper.

"Why?"

"All Rose does is push me around. Does anyone

ever ask me for advice? Oh, no. She doesn't give me any respect. It's not fair."

"Does Rose have a boss?"

"Yes. The founder of The Three Circles Society is her boss but he's long dead by now."

"Oh."

"He died in 1992. That was the year that Alice Carter was Head until Rose took over a few years on and to this day she hasn't changed a bit."

"Why isn't Alice Carter her boss?"

"Because she disappeared in the dead of night and hasn't come back since."

"What age is Rose?"

"Forty-nine."

"OK. What age are you?"

"Forty-two."

"So you're seven years younger than her."

"Yes, and if you don't mind me asking, what age are you?"

"Thirty and a bit. My brother's twenty-nine."

"OK. Is that him there?"

JJ pointed to Paolo.

"Yeah. That's Paolo."

"Hey, if you're Italian, how can you speak English?"

"Our mother is Irish."

"Ah. Do you know how to speak Italian?"

"Absolutely!"

JJ Bines didn't say anything else and Paolo shouted to the men to join the group heading to the car. There was never going to be room for everyone!

They had reached the blue Bentley. JJ hopped into the car with the usual suspects and the Bentley trudged off.

"So you're going to stay with us for a while, eh, JJ?" said Dave from the driver's seat.

"Um…yeah, suppose."

"And you're gonna help on the Dawn Hughes case,

right?"

"Something like that, yeah."

"Cool."

The Bentley moved forward. It was a very cold day and practically everyone was wearing coats but still shivering like crazy.

When they pulled up at The New Yorker Hotel, it was half past six. "Hey, anyone up for dinner?" asked Dave, as they made their way to the cellar ladder.

"Yes please," said Vivian and Daniel, speaking for everyone.

So they went out for dinner in suits and a dress – obviously Vivian's – to a different restaurant, The Mona Lisa, which wasn't a pizzeria.

Paolo loved that restaurant. He loved it because the staff were nice and the atmosphere was beautiful. Everyone was talking and noise filled the entire restaurant. He liked the tables, the chairs, the waiters, the food (especially the food!) and he loved pretty much everything else.

The group ate in silence for the fifty minutes. Complete silence, but in their heads each one was thinking about their next step and they all knew they were refuelling for battle.

Just before it was time to leave the restaurant, a strange figure came out away from the bar, no one had noticed him before, each one being caught up in his or her own thoughts. He was wearing a shiny purple coat, and had a scar running across his face. He also wore a smug expression.

He walked to the table and stood, staring at Dave. "Nice to see you, David," he said.

"Not nice to see you too, Victor."

Victor chuckled. "I'm sure it isn't, my old friend."

"Friend?" said Vivian in disbelief, staring at Dave.

"Oh, yes we were once in college together. The best of friends," chuckled Victor.

"I was not your friend and if I was I'd regret it!"

"Well, well, well. I bet you won't regret it when I take over the world." He was taunting them and they knew what he had done.

"You never will! I don't know why you had to turn evil in the FIRST PLACE!"

Dave was standing now, glaring at Victor, who

simply shrugged and said, "I'll see you at the end of the world. And then who'll be laughing? Me."

And with that, Victor Left sashayed out of the restaurant, turned a corner, and left the gang.

"You were friends with Victor Left?" cried Vivian when he had left.

"It was before I joined The Three Circles and we weren't real friends!"

"What was he like when he was younger?"

"Nice enough. He thought I was his best friend. I felt sorry for him. So I decided to team up with him. I'm sorry."

He looked meaningfully at Vivian. "I mean it. Seriously."

"OK, but please don't give me such a fright again Dad."

This is when the secret came out. That last word. Dad. Dave was Vivian's father? This led to surprised expressions, questions bubbling up inside of people. Though there was one question that truly outshone the others.

If Dave was Vivian's dad then who was Vivian's

mother?

Straight to the point and as curious as everyone else Daniel simply decided to ask.

"Well, Angeline is," said Dave. "She's out working as a volunteer on housing projects in Africa. She's a nurse. We're still a happily married couple though. She's coming home in a couple of months."

"Well, that's good, right?" said Paolo.

"Yes. And no."

"Why?"

"She kind of… doesn't really know about The Three Circles."

"What?!"

"You have to tell her Dad," said Vivian anxiously. "We've been here before."

"I just don't see why she needs to know right now – you know how she worries."

"Tell her!" shouted Giuseppe much to everyone's surprise but after which they all joined in.

"Tell her, tell her, tell her!" they all chanted until

Dave got up from the table.

"Ok," he sighed. "I will tell her on the phone now."

The he took out his iPhone and dialled a number.

"Hi Angeline."

A pause.

"Good. I'm good, but before you say any more there's something I'd like to tell you."

Then he explained everything.

There were some long pauses, Dave's face went red and he apologised over and over.

"Please don't be mad," he was saying. "I just didn't want to worry you."

"Yes I know she is only fifteen but she's very mature and a great asset to the society…" Vivian was beaming and Dave winked at her.

Sighing again he said, "Angeline I'm sorry but trust me this is a really good place for her to be and she's by my side all of the time. We are a team and when you come home you will join us."

There was a long pause and no one seemed to be

saying anything. The room was filled with tension and Dave seemed to be waiting for something....until he could hold his breath no longer.

"I'm sorry," he said again.

Another pause.

Then his face was lighting up.... "So you're OK with it?!"

"Yahoo!"

Another pause.

"Yes, yes, I promise to look after her..."

"Yes and me too!" He was laughing now and with that everyone cheered, Vivian jumped up and before he could hang up she hugged Dave and shouted, "Love you Mum!"

CHAPTER 9

Green turns Purple

It was late at night. Three days had passed since Dawn had been put into that cramped little cell in Southern Brooklyn. Two days since her last discussion with Victor Left.

She thought of those two Italian magicians. What were their names? She couldn't remember. She shook it off. It didn't matter now.

She was tired and felt so drained. At least she was still able to eat beautifully rich food, and was allowed to run around once every day in the beautiful flower garden – which seemed so out of place for the city. Eventually though she got thrown back into the cell.

Three days – nearly four by her estimation. She didn't know where she was, though she presumed she was in Brooklyn. When she was let out she could see the lights shining brightly.

Suddenly Dawn's thoughts were interrupted when the door to her cell swung open and Victor Left walked in. He wasn't alone.

Standing next to him, all shackled up – was a black-haired lady in ripped clothes. She struggled to get unshackled but it didn't work.

Then she was thrown into the cell opposite Dawn.

He really was gone bad.

*

The atmosphere was nervous in Mahogany Castle. Though it was 11.30pm the gang had no intention of sleeping. They had too much on their minds – what was the plan? This seemed to be the most-asked question.

They didn't have one apart from storm the store. They sat there, in the weapons room, trying to think of something, but nothing came. Did they need it to be elaborate? What if the kidnappers panicked – who knows what they would do?

Then there was a knock on the door. At this hour, it was peculiar.

"Come in," said Dave stepping aside to let the men in the grey suits scuttle through the doorway.

As the last man shut the door behind him, Dave asked, "What's the matter?"

"Well, there are many things that are the matter in life. People… how do I put this … eh… people have sides. Let's just get this done with."

Then something very strange and terrible happened. The men's suits turned purple.

"Oh my God."

"Oh sweet Lord."

"Oh, no."

"Oh, that's just great."

"Hello, David," said the first man.

"Hello, Mr Carling."

"Long time no see."

"Best for both of us."

"I'm going to try and kill you now."

"Go ahead."

"Just try and stop me!"

Then Mr Carling lunged at Dave, who simply stepped out of the way and watched the man fall to the ground.

"Ah, Alexander Carling. You've lost your magic touch."

Within a second Dave was pinned down with a dagger about two centimetres from his heart.

"If you try to kill me for the fifteenth time in three years – oh yes I'm counting – and if you succeed, I have back up. In case you haven't noticed – we are in the weapons room, where all the weapons are stored. If you dare even so much as touch my shirt I – or someone else – will strangle you to death. So I suggest you get off of me."

Slowly, Carling stood up. "I'll let it go this time, David Brackett!" he shouted loudly. He was obviously completely stupid because this attracted the rest of the occupants of the castle.

Rose made her way to the front. "I am arresting you under the charges of assaulting a fully trained and classified agent. I know that you work for Left, but you will be kept here for the time being."

"But…what?" Alexander Carling protested but Rose wasn't having any of it. "You will be kept here until there is FURTHER NOTICE!" she yelled at the men.

They were led to the underground dungeon and locked in a large cell, with rats scuttling around like mad things.

Paolo and Giuseppe, who had followed the escort down just to be sure they were locked away, walked back up the dungeon stairs to be greeted by Vivian and Dave.

"So you're quite the fighter," said Giuseppe. He and Dave were walking ahead of the rest.

"What do you mean?"

"That guy tried to kill you and you stopped him."

"Oh, Carling. Oh he's always been trying to kill me. He despises of me. He tries to murder a lot of people, and I am second on his most wanted list."

"Who's first?"

"Probably a woman named Victoria Richards. She is not intertwined with The Three Circles, but not with the Purple Army either. She works for no one. She lives with her sister and is dangerous because there is one thing that Victoria Richards has that no one else does. She has magic."

"Ahem?" Giuseppe was looking quite offended.

"Yes magic," Dave didn't seem to get what Giuseppe the MAGICIAN was getting at!

He kept talking. "It started off as simple things – household things and that, but then her thirst for power led her to become a sorceress. The most powerful things they are, a bloodthirsty lot. There are only about thirty of them left. There were thirty-one though. I'll tell you how the other one died. I saw it."

Giuseppe forgot about being offended. "Tell me!" he said.

"Well, it was a couple of decades ago. I was twenty-something and was sitting on a bench at around 11pm. This bench looked over onto a beach. No one was at this beach until suddenly a red light flashed right in front of me and I saw two men wearing cloaks.

"The one wearing the green cloak gave a smug grin. Then the one who was wearing blue started to shiver. I thought he was just cold – it was winter. It turned out that it was a spell coming along. Then there was a black light that went from the blue man's hand to the green man's heart and the green man dropped to the ground dead. Then the blue man came over to me and looked me in the eye"….Dave's mind wandered for a moment before he added: "There is a whole world in ours full of monstrous creatures, sorcerers, dragons, wizards and people like Left and Carling."

"Do you have magic?" asked Giuseppe.

"A little bit. I'll teach you my kind of magic if you like. What colour is your blood?"

"Red, like everyone."

"If you say that, it's definitely white. Self-belief is the thing you don't want to have if you want magic."

"What? Isn't that kind of… strange?"

"Sort of. But then again… magic is strange, you know?"

"Very true but I am a magician."

"Yes you are, but that's fake magic."

"What!" Giuseppe was feeling offended again.

"They are just tricks but I'm not talking tricks. I'm talking about spell books, powers and potions. I'm talking about real magic."

Giuseppe was too intrigued to argue, he wanted to know more, but they had reached the grand entrance of Mahogany Castle so the conversation had to come to an end for now. They sat down on the bench. It was 1.29am. They had a minute to prepare before they would meet JJ, Cook, Sinbad (who had decided he was bothered after all!) and another man for a discussion on the Dawn Hughes front.

Within seconds they entered the room quietly, striding in without even a hint of the slightest whisper.

"Hello," said Dave.

"Hello, Dave," said Sinbad, who was at the front of the small line that they had assembled.

"Would you like to host this meeting here, or in Room Five?"

"I think we should do it right here." Sinbad winked at Dave, and Dave nodded.

Paolo did not know what exactly this meant.

CHAPTER 10

The Phone Call

"It was a sunny summer's day in Chile, along the coast. I was walking along, minding my own business, when I heard someone walking behind me. Then I turned and saw who it was. It was Victoria Richards. She stared at me for three seconds. Three seconds was all it took. She was hypnotising me, don't you see? Soldiers were after her. They were magical. So she made me beat them up and protect her but I did something else. I killed a man. I killed one of the soldiers but I refuse to call myself a murderer – it was Victoria Richards. She was the murderer. She is too powerful. Way too powerful."

"And I met her again, in Bahrain, recently. I was disguised as a tour guide off work but visiting the site of Albatross Castle. Then she just… appeared. Right in front of me. It took me a few seconds to realise who it was. I was next to a stream, which she threw me in. Soldiers, the same ones, were searching again. I think she stole water and they thought I had done it. She is horrible. I rest my case," said Mr Browne, the man behind Sinbad.

"But I think she can help us," replied Dave. "She has magic. It's vital."

"I know, but just to tell you, she's wretched. She won't want to come. If she does, she either wants to kill us, Dawn or Victor but we'll contact her."

"Yes. Does everyone agree with this?"

There were nods all around the room. "Good. We'll call her straight away."

Dave stood up and walked to the telephone. He waited thirty seconds before saying, "It's been a long time, Vic."

"Yes it has."

"You got me into a lot of scrapes and trouble I shouldn't have been in."

"I like to live a dangerous life."

"Listen. We need your help. Kidnapping. Ever heard of that Dawn Hughes lady?"

"Yeah, I generally like to keep up with the Arts. I'm smart."

"That's great. Well, she's the one who's been kidnapped."

"I'm guessing stolen by Left in yet another attempt to take over the world! He thinks he's more powerful than the Grand Sorcerer," she sneered. "So what kind of help?"

"Magical help."

"Ah." Though Dave could not see her, he knew that she was smiling. She couldn't resist showing off and he knew she would say yes.

"I'll meet you outside Mahogany Castle at 2.30am."

"Goodbye."

Dave hung up. "We meet around the back."

Mr Browne showed horror in his face. "Victoria Richards? Answering you? Telling you yes? I don't think so."

"Well think again, Mr Browne," said Dave.

"But… she's…but…"

"NO BUTS, BROWNE!" shouted Dave and it ended the matter.

About half an hour later, the gang walked out of Mahogany Castle and around the back. She was waiting.

Victoria Richards had beautiful black hair that nearly reached her legs. She wore a white dress and looked like a Russian doll. Her face was amazing – she was the most beautiful woman Paolo had ever set eyes on.

"Hello, David," she said, her voice cold and strong, giving a quick nod of her head. She looked surprised to see how many people had shown up.

"That's a lot of mortals. So I hear you've got Alexander Carling and the Nirlan Brothers locked up in that little castle of yours," said Victoria.

"Yes, but more importantly Dawn Hughes is missing. Victor Left has done it again."

Victoria shook her head and said "Tut, tut. I think he's gone mad, I really do."

"I'm sure you do, but insane or completely healthy, he's captured Dawn Hughes."

"So you need my help."

"Yes."

Victoria laughed. "I remember, on the 18th of September, Dave Brackett told me that he would never need my, or anyone else's, help ever again."

"That was a wrong choice. I'm sorry. Now come on. Will you do it or not?"

"I'll do it."

"Good. Stay the night here."

"No. I'll sleep in the woods."

"You truly are crazy, aren't you?"

"Yes. Now goodbye."

"I'll see you in the morning at Mahogany Woods."

CHAPTER 11

The Sixteenth Attempt

As the sun rose, outside the dungeons of Mahogany Castle, Alexander Carling was fighting for his life. Opposite him and also trying to get him killed was Rose Dahlia. He ducked a blow that would have sent him knocking backwards.

Then he turned for the exit and ran. Since it was early morning, the shifts for guards were just changing. Fortunately for Carling, there was no one guarding the dungeon so he kept on running, knocking over tables and chairs as he went. Rounding the corridor he tripped on something and stumbled to the floor.

Rose ran in just as he regained consciousness. She laughed and said, "I win."

Then Alexander Carling hopped back up and began to run again. Sprinting around the corridors was dangerous, so he took refuge, when he eventually got upstairs, in Room Five. He hid under the meeting table.

Rose, Mr Browne and some other agents passed Room Five without a notice. Alexander grinned. His assistants were all dead – killed by either Mr Browne or Rose Dahlia but he was better than that.

It was all over. He had won. He could leave this place and go back to Left and he would be upgraded in his ranking to Deputy.

Then there came something Carling wasn't expecting. Dave, Paolo, Giuseppe, Daniel and Vivian walked into Room Five.

At first Alexander looked at it as a negative but then he had a different idea. He would break out and tackle Dave – and the others if necessary. Surely the other agents wouldn't hear him. Well not if he made his move quietly – but he couldn't do that.

Without giving a second thought, Alexander Carling leapt out from under the table with a deafening "ARGH!" and jumped on Dave, who was knocked over before he knew what was happening.

Carling had Dave pinned down. This was it. This was his final chance. He searched for his dagger in his coat pocket, forgetting about Dave who took the opportunity to throw a punch, that had just about enough force to get Carling off of him, and allow him to join the others who had all formed a circle around Carling and were closing in.

At last it was the end for Alexander Carling.

*

Dawn Hughes was starting to get scared. Scared that Victor Left had changed his mind and was actually going to harm her. Scared that everything would go wrong and no one would rescue her. She imagined this but tried her best to steer her mind clear of the subject.

*

As Dave stepped over Alexander Carling, Vivian spotted something odd... Carling was still alive.

Vivian didn't have time to think before he jumped back up, kicked Dave in the thighs and ran out of the room. He kept running up the hallway and out of Mahogany Castle before anyone could catch him. In the courtyard, he ran to a Volvo, which he jumped into and sped off in.

Dave, Vivian, Daniel and the Fragola brothers ran to Rose. "He's got away!" they screamed and shouted.

"Too late," said Rose coming up behind them.

"No it isn't! We can still catch him!" complained Vivian.

"Yes it is. He'll go back to Victor Left and it's not

my problem."

"Yes it is! You horrible little brat!"

As soon as the words slipped out of Vivian Brackett's mouth, she suddenly regretted it. She ran down the hall but Rose didn't follow.

"What do you think you're doing?" shouted Dave angrily at Vivian.

"Dad, I was just mad. Let it go."

"Fine but this isn't over."

The gang paraded back down the hallway, through the grand entrance and out to the blue Bentley, located in the courtyard, where they set off.

CHAPTER 12

Victoria Richards

When the Bentley slowed to a halt Paolo, Giuseppe, Vivian and Daniel hopped out, closely followed by Dave.

They looked around in the morning frost and then began, slowly, to walk into the woods.

The pine trees were evergreens. There were occasional rustling sounds and Paolo could have sworn he saw a rat. Then out strode Victoria Richards, in a blue dress this time. She was still captivatingly beautiful.

"You're here, I see." She had the same tone as last time – cold with a hint of evil.

"Yes, we are. Can we get down to business, or are you just going to wait here?" answered Dave, quite smartly.

"Fine, fine."

"We want you to come with us to South Brooklyn. Carling escaped. He'll go back to Victor. We have to have you there. It's our only hope."

"I'll do it,"

"Yes!"

"…At a cost."

"Oh."

"Here's the catch. I want to be able to kill Victor Left."

"You can do whatever you like with him. He's yours for the keeping, darling. As long as you help us."

"One – don't call me darling – it's really annoying. Two – I hate helping people and three, I'll do it but only this time, Brackett!"

"Yes!"

"I'll pick the day."

"Don't push your luck! We're leaving now."

It looked like she was going to say something, not being used to being told what to do, but Dave simply turned his back on her and made for the car.

CHAPTER 13

Deepwater Cottage

The Blue Bentley pulled up at a road near an abandoned estate. Most of the houses were burned down. There was no sense of life. Victoria Richards, from the front passenger seat, navigated the car, which was swerving in between pieces of wood and rubbish.

About forty years ago, she explained, an evil sorcerer destroyed this estate. A lot of magical people lived there.

"Take a left," she said. "Now stop. Here we are."

The only house that had not been attacked was painted black with every blind in every window drawn. Dead flowers in flowerpots lay at the door.

Victoria held her hand out. A bright green light illuminated the doorknob and her left hand and the door swung open. "It's protected by a Shield. Shields are hard to make. I've only made one. They take months to finish. Come on, you can walk in."

Deepwater Cottage was filled with old artefacts and was filled with musty aromas. Paolo and Giuseppe followed Vivian, who knew the place like the back of her hand. There were traps everywhere she said - one wrong move and they could die.

"Now. Enter this room," demanded Vivian.

At the end of the dangerous hall there lay a door with a silver doorknob. Victoria muttered something quickly and the door exploded.

"Oh great! I always get that spell wrong." Then she muttered something else and the door repaired itself. She pulled on the doorknob and the door opened.

Inside the room there was a settee and seven armchairs. There was also a mahogany desk with a laptop lying on it. Vials of different-coloured liquid were packed up in small open boxes. Lying on the desk next to the laptop was a china tea set. "Let's discuss the plan over tea," said Victoria, and took a seat in one of the armchairs.

Gradually each member of the group sat down in the chairs. They were comfy.

Victoria stood and walked over to a blank space of wall. Hanging from the roof was a cord. She tugged on it and a huge piece of blueprint fell down quickly.

"What is that?" said Daniel, in amazement.

"This is our plan. Now listen carefully."

The plan was complicated. Very, very complicated. There was a lot of running around, digging tunnels and trickery so by the time she had reached the end of her explanation Giuseppe's jaw had dropped.

"One word – improvisation!" said Dave. We should not go through with this plan! It's too complicated!"

"No it's not!" exclaimed Victoria, quite offended by the remark.

"Yes it is!"

"Is not."

"Is so!"

"PEOPLE! You're acting like schoolchildren," interrupted Vivian.

"Yes, you are and you're giving me a headache," added Giuseppe.

"Is so," mumbled Dave quietly after the discussion was finished. Victoria did hear but she didn't want to start all over again so she remained quiet, simply scowling in Dave's direction.

"We'll just improvise," said Vivian quietly bringing

the situation to a conclusion. "It's OK. We have a lot of people. The only thing is – people will see us. They will know who we are and the society will be revealed."

"Oh great," said Daniel.

"That's just what we need," said Dave sarcastically.

"Oh come on, no one will see us. Lighten up. Let's get it over and done with! Someone's life is on the line!" shouted Victoria.

"Yeah, Victoria's right!" said Giuseppe.

"Yeah, Giuseppe and Victoria are completely correct!" exclaimed Paolo, standing up.

Daniel stood up. "I believe we can do it!"

"So do I!" shouted Vivian joining him. Her eyes rested on Dave, who shrugged and asked, "What else have we to lose?" and stood up.

"LET'S SHOW THEM WHAT WE'RE MADE OF!" the gang shouted in unison.

Then they put their hands in a group and said "AARRRRRRRRGGGGGGGGGGGHHHHH!"

Finally, they were down to business.

CHAPTER 14

The Grand Finale

The Bentley was packed. Sitting in the car were Dave, Paolo, Giuseppe, Vivian, Daniel and the Sorcerer Victoria Richards. The rest of the gang had been contacted and were meeting them at the location.

About an hour later, they arrived in Brooklyn. The Bentley pulled up on a street outside the run-down shop. They were ready for battle.

The shop had been for let for six months. Someone took it. One of The Purple Army's associates. The Purple Army then used the place as one of its worldwide secret bases. It was brilliant – no one would think for a minute that a secret society was operating there.

As the gang walked towards the building, Victoria spotted Alexander Carling striding along. "CHARGE!" they all shouted.

*

Dawn Hughes heard footsteps. Then a man ran in.

He was being chased. He tripped and fell and the keys he had in his hands fell to the floor – they were the keys to the cells.

The people who were chasing him smiled and one of the men picked the keys up before shouting, "Grab her!" and throwing them to a pretty young girl as he pointed at Dawn.

"Come with us," said the girl to Dawn. "We're the good guys," but she never made it to the door.

As they were fidgeting around with the keys Victor Left ran into the room, along with several other Purple Army members.

Victoria turned all her intentions on him. She sent a fireball blazing towards him. He ducked and then lunged at her and she went flying backwards.

It was a tough fight – Victoria just ahead. It crossed her mind, as they fought, that Victor had once hoped to be a sorcerer but he only just made it to wizard level – she allowed herself a sneer. He just wasn't up to her capabilities.

Victor snapped his hands and a green light shot at Victoria. She muttered something under her breath and a red bolt went straight at the green light.

The red bolt enveloped the green light, but the

green light fought back. Victoria's spell was stronger, however, and the red bolt caused the green light to disintegrate as Victor dropped, at the same time, to the ground, unconscious.

Dave was fighting Alexander. It was a tough match. Alexander had a large stick and Dave just had his bare hands. The fight was in full swing but Carling was winning.

Paolo, who was being chased by several members of the Purple Army jumped up and onto a cramped window ledge from where he watched as Alexander Carling fell to the ground and lost out to Dave. All around the cramped corridor Purple Army members had descended and were taking on The Three Circles society members and volunteers.

Bottles were being smashed, people were shouting and all around them magic – but not as he'd known it – was being used. He was in awe, but no more so than when he caught a glimpse of his brother, Vivian and Daniel use nothing but eye contact to formulate the move that would end everything.

Daniel, who had just tripped up a Purple Army agent, had noticed the keys he had picked up minutes before, back in Dave's pocket. As Dave battled with Carling Daniel ran by, slipped the keys out and winking at Giuseppe, who had just freed himself of a very strong looking woman agent of the enemy, slid the bunch across the floor. Giuseppe stopped the keys with his foot and scooped them up, whistling at the same time to get the attention of Vivian who was tying an agent's hand behind his back. As she looked up Giuseppe threw the keys in her direction and being nearest to the cell door she bolted for it.

Just as the key turned there was a loud shriek from the centre of the room where Victor Left had his arms wrapped around his own neck it what looked like a very strange spell.

"You will remain like that until you change your ways," Victoria was shouting. "Now be gone, all of you unless you want to risk ending up like that too!"

"I call off the Purple Army," said Victor miserably. "You can all go home. This isn't a joke. Goodbye everyone, I'm leaving!" And despite his pleading eyes Victoria turned her back on him and everyone, including Alexander Carling, fled the room.

A loud cheer brightened up the depressing surroundings as Dawn Hughes finally exited her cell and thanked everyone ten times. The Three Circles society had won, they had saved the day...well ok they had a little help from the sorcerer...

It was only then that they discovered, as they turned around to settle their differences and thank her, that the red plume of smoke in the middle of the room was the signal that she had gone.

*

Dawn was dropped off at 23rd Grange and Paolo and Giuseppe booked tickets for a flight back to Venice. They had had enough of New York.

The Bentley bumped along to LaGuardia airport. It was early in the morning and they got a parking spot. The gang hopped out of the car.

"I'm gonna miss you, Paolo and Giuseppe," said an almost teary-eyed Vivian.

"We all are," shouted Dave and Daniel.

"Goodbye Paolo! Goodbye Giuseppe! Sorry that your New York career didn't get off to a great start."

"Goodbye everyone!"

And with that, The Fragola Brothers walked towards the airport, acutely aware that they had only managed one magic show since they got there.